Seymour Simon

SEE MORE READERS

AMAZING BATS

SeaStar Books · San Francisco

For Joel and Benjamin Simon
and Chloe and Jeremy Simon
with love from Grandpa Seymour

Permission to use the following photographs is gratefully acknowledged:

Front cover: © Joe McDonald/Bruce Coleman Inc.; Front cover spot photograph © Jane Burton/Bruce Coleman Inc.; title page: © B. G. Thomson/Photo Researchers; pages 2–3: © B. G. Thomson/Photo Researchers; page 4 © Dr. Merlin Tuttle/Photo Researchers; page 5: © Michael Fogden/Bruce Coleman Inc.; pages 6–7: © Dr. Merlin Tuttle/Photo Researchers; pages 8–9: © Dr. Merlin Tuttle/BCI/Photo Researchers; pages 10–11: © Mark Sherman/Bruce Coleman Inc.; pages 12–13: © Jacana/Photo Researchers; pages 14–15: © Michael Fogden/AnimalsAnimals; pages 16–17: © Dr. Merlin Tuttle/Photo Researchers; pages 18–19: © Frederick R. McConnaughey/Photo Researchers; pages 20–21: © Michael Fogden/Bruce Coleman Inc; pages 22–23: © Carrie Robertson/Bat Conservation Internatioinal/Photo Researchers; pages 24–25: © B. G. Thomson/Photo Researchers; pages 26–27: © W. Perry Conway/CORBIS; pages 28–29: © Sdeuard Bisserot/Bruce Coleman Inc; pages 30–31: © Stephen Dalton/Photo Researchers; page 32 © Jane Burton/Bruce Coleman Inc.; back cover: © Dr. Merlin Tuttle/BCI/Photo Researchers

Book design by E. Friedman.
Typeset in 22-point ITC Century Book.
Manufactured in China.

SeaStar is an imprint of Chronicle Books LLC.

Library of Congress Cataloging-in-Publication Data
Simon, Seymour.
Amazing Bats / Seymour Simon.
p. cm. — (SeeMore readers)
ISBN 1-58717-261-5 (library binding)
ISBN 1-58717-262-3 (paperback)
1. Bats — Juvenile literature. I. Title
QL737.C5S55 2005
599.4—dc22
2004023621

Distributed in Canada by Raincoast Books
9050 Shaughnessy Street, Vancouver, British Columbia V6P 6E5

10 9 8 7 6 5 4 3 2 1

Chronicle Books LLC
85 Second Street, San Francisco, California 94105

www.chroniclekids.com

Bats are the only mammals that can fly.

Bat wings look like hands with skin stretched between the long fingers.

The scientific name for bats means "hand-wing."

There are about a thousand kinds of bats.

They live all around the world.

About 45 kinds of bats live in the United States.

Some bats live in caves throughout the year. Other bats live in trees and under roofs during the summer and in caves during the winter. They hang upside down on the cave ceiling and come out at night to eat.

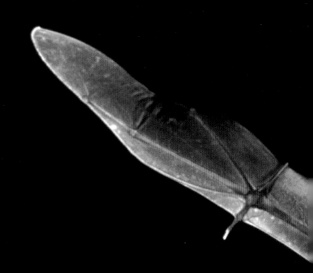

Most bats eat insects.

A little brown bat can eat
about 600 bugs an hour.

That's like you eating 20
pizzas a night!

A small colony of bats can
eat a ton of insects in one year.

That's more than 600 million bugs.

Other bats eat ripe fruit and sweet liquid from flowers. Fruit bats are large and have powerful teeth and jaws they use to bite off pieces of food.

Fruit bats nest in trees, and most kinds come out only at night to feed.

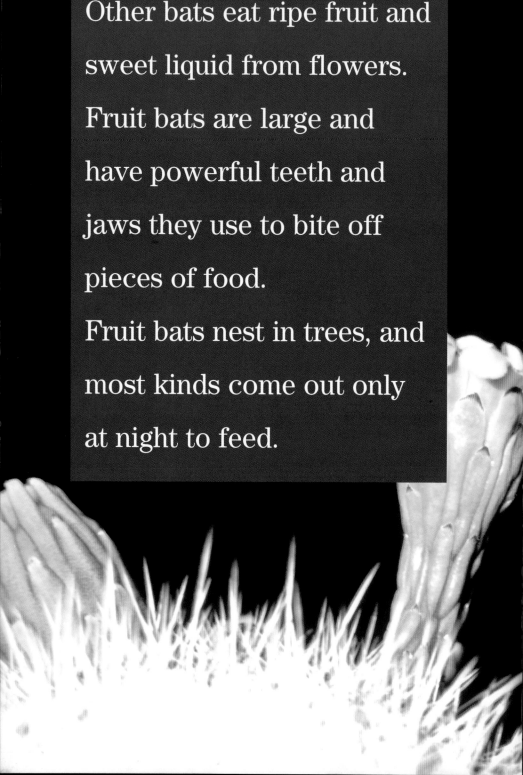

Some bats eat small fishes
or frogs.
A frog-eating bat, in Panama,
swoops down on its victim
and carries it off.

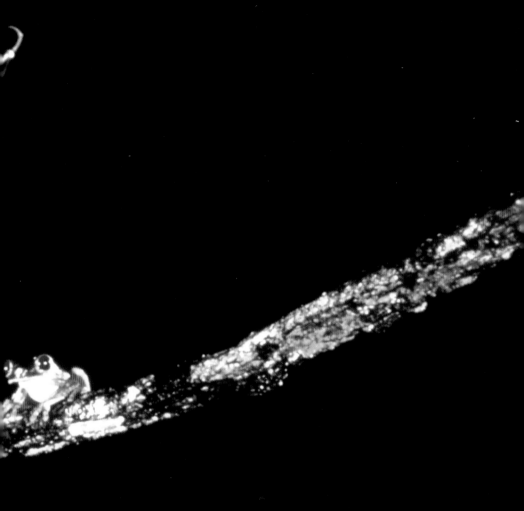

The bat finds its meal by listening

for the sounds of male frogs

croaking.

The bat can tell if the frog is the

right size by the sounds it makes.

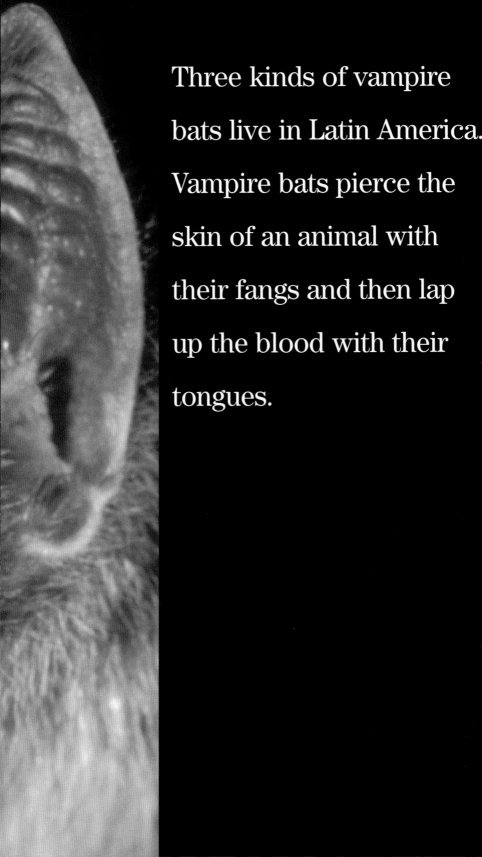

Three kinds of vampire bats live in Latin America. Vampire bats pierce the skin of an animal with their fangs and then lap up the blood with their tongues.

In winter, when there are fewer fruits, flowers, and flying insects for bats to eat, some bats travel to warmer places.

Millions of free-tailed bats spend summers in Texas and New Mexico. In winter, free-tailed bats travel hundreds of miles south to feeding spots in Mexico.

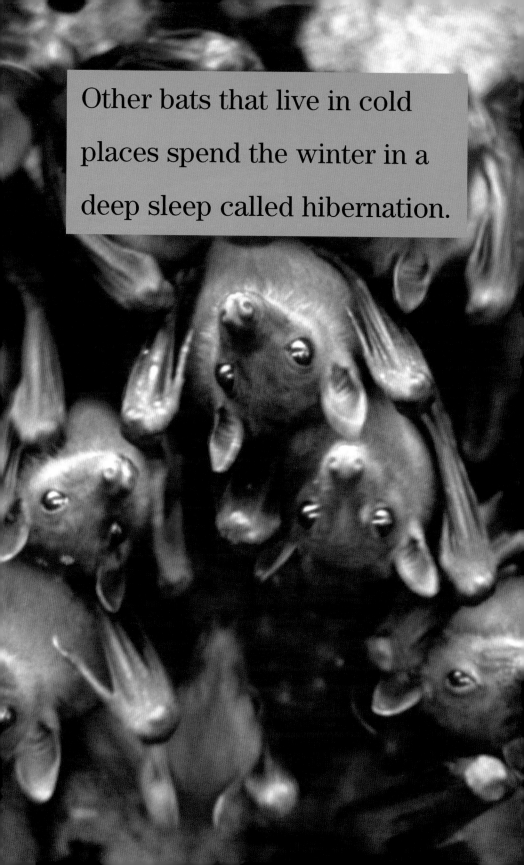

Other bats that live in cold places spend the winter in a deep sleep called hibernation.

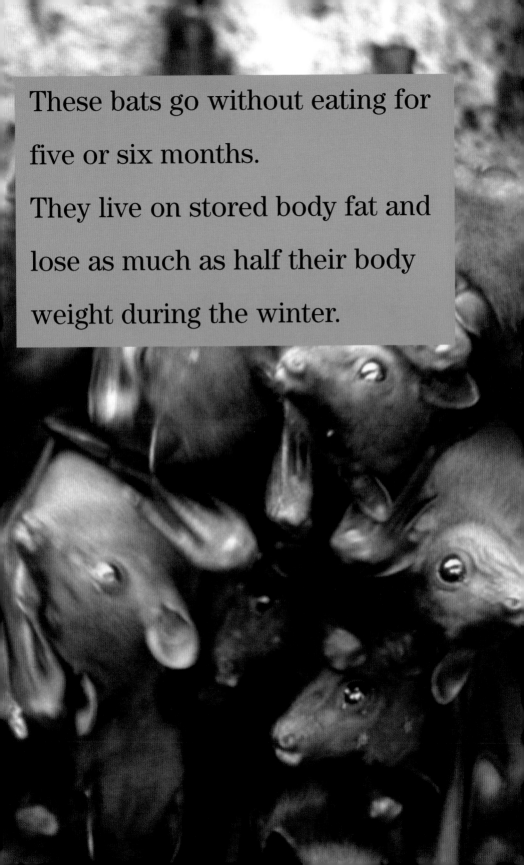

These bats go without eating for five or six months.

They live on stored body fat and lose as much as half their body weight during the winter.

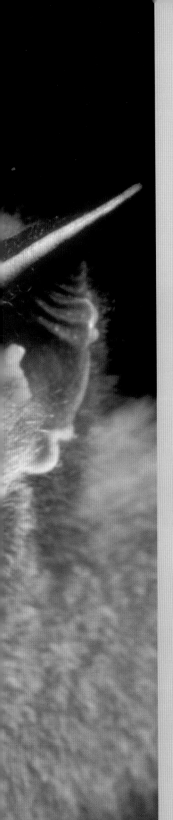

Many stories about bats are untrue. For example, bats are not blind. Many bats can see very well. Bats also use sound echoes called sonar to locate insects and other foods.

Some people are afraid of bats. But bats do not attack people. And bats will not get tangled up in your hair.

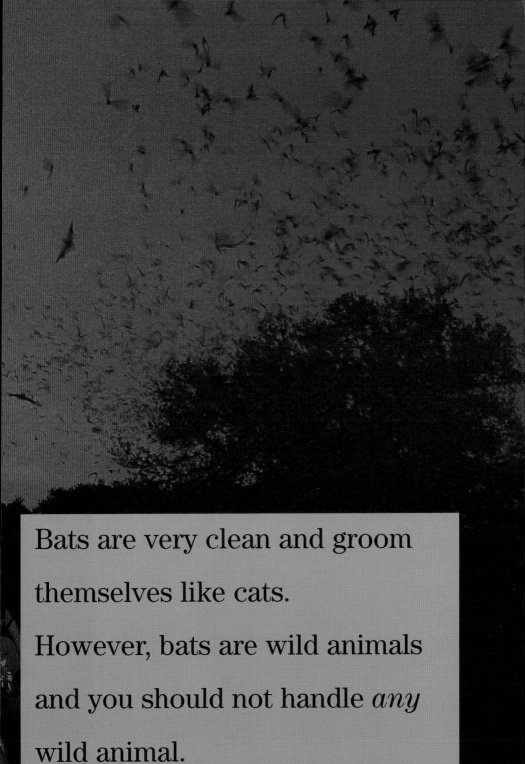

Bats are very clean and groom themselves like cats.

However, bats are wild animals and you should not handle *any* wild animal.

All bats belong to one of two groups, megabats and microbats. Megabats are large bats that live in warm climates and eat fruits. Microbats are small, insect-eating bats found all over the world, including the United States.

The biggest bat in the world is
called the gigantic flying fox,
from Asia.

It weighs more than 2 pounds and
has a wingspan of 6 feet.

That's wider than you are tall.
The gigantic flying fox eats
only fruit—and it eats lots!

One of the smallest
and commonest bats in the
world is called the pipistrelle
(pip-uh-STRELL).
It weighs less than two
pennies and is only as long
as your little finger.
But the tiny pipistrelle can eat
3,000 insects in just one night.

Actual Size

The Australian ghost bat can swoop down and carry away a mouse for food.

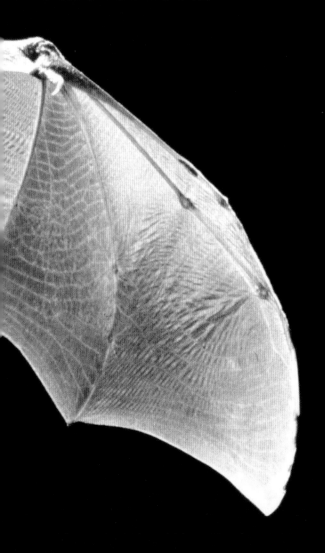

Bats help keep you free of mosquitoes and other insect bites. Bats don't harm people—they help them.

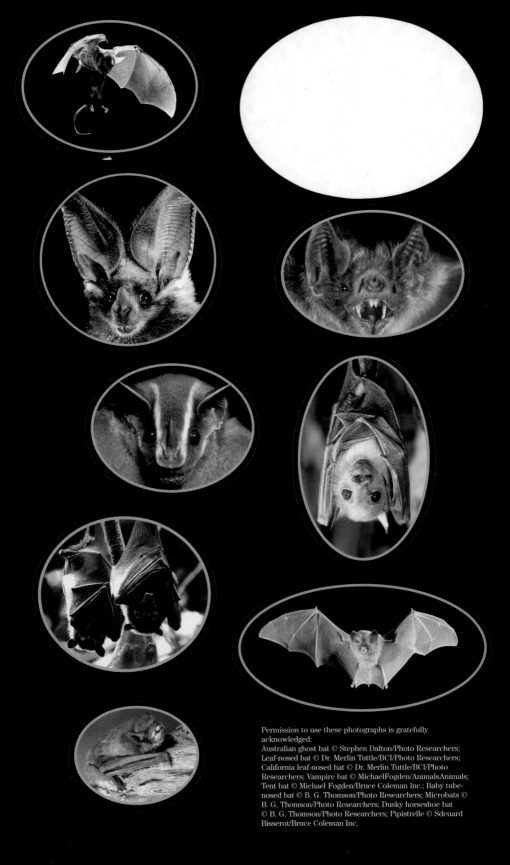

Permission to use these photographs is gratefully acknowledged:
Australian ghost bat © Stephen Dalton/Photo Researchers;
Leaf-nosed bat © Dr. Merlin Tuttle/BCI/Photo Researchers;
California leaf-nosed bat © Dr. Merlin Tuttle/BCI/Photo
Researchers; Vampire bat © MichaelFogden/AnimalsAnimals;
Tent bat © Michael Fogden/Bruce Coleman Inc.; Baby tube-
nosed bat © B. G. Thomson/Photo Researchers; Microbats ©
B. G. Thomson/Photo Researchers; Dusky horseshoe bat
© B. G. Thomson/Photo Researchers; Pipistrelle © Sdeuard
Bisserot/Bruce Coleman Inc.